Into the Riverlands

Into the Riverlands

NGHI VO

A TOM DOHERTY ASSOCIATES BOOK
NEW YORK

INTO THE RIVERLANDS

A Tordotcom Book
Published by Tom Doherty Associates
120 Broadway
New York, NY 10271

www.tor.com

Tor® is a registered trademark of Macmillan Publishing Group, LLC.

Library of Congress Cataloging-in-Publication Data

Names: Vo, Nghi, author.
Title: Into the riverlands / Nghi Vo.
Description: First edition. | New York : Tordotcom, 2022. | Series:
    The Singing Hills cycle ; 3 | "A Tom Doherty Associates book."
Identifiers: LCCN 2022021022 (print) | LCCN 2022021023 (ebook) |
    ISBN 9781250851420 (hardcover) | ISBN 9781250837998 (ebook)
Subjects: LCGFT: Novellas.
Classification: LCC PS3622.O23 I58 2022 (print) | LCC PS3622.O23
    (ebook) | DDC 813/.6—dc23/eng/20220502
LC record available at https://lccn.loc.gov/2022021022
LC ebook record available at https://lccn.loc.gov/2022021023

Our books may be purchased in bulk for promotional, educational,
or business use. Please contact your local bookseller or the Macmillan
Corporate and Premium Sales Department at 1-800-221-7945, extension
5442, or by email at MacmillanSpecialMarkets@macmillan.com.

First Edition: 2022

Printed in the United States of America

0 9 8 7 6 5 4 3 2 1

for Carolyn

Into the Riverlands

Chapter One

The barber paused, flicking water droplets from his razor with a brisk snap of his wrist.

"Well, I once shaved Governor Liu of Qin Province during the processional, and last summer, I stepped in to thread Crimson Bow's brows when her own barber was ill."

"Crimson Bow, the actress from Fenghua?" asked Chih with interest, and the barber made a humming noise of assent as he rubbed a little more oil into their scalp. The first slide of the razor against Chih's head sent a not altogether pleasant shiver through their body, but they took a deep breath and sat as still as it was advisable to sit when a large man held an enormous sharp razor that close to their face.

"Yeah. Her company, the Resplendent Sky-whatever, they were touring up through Vihn. They were doing that play, you know, the one about the marriage of that sect leader in the down-country."

Chih sat very straight as the barber recounted the plot of *The Cruel Wife of Master See,* because after all, reviews and criticisms were their own kind of history, but the quick rhythmic movements of the barber's razor put them into something of a daze. The sharp blade glided over the curves of their scalp as if it intimately knew every bump and hollow, and the tingles that always ran up Chih's spine and, for some reason, behind their knees, when they got their head shorn gradually took up all of their attention.

It seemed no time at all before the barber whipped the old muslin cape off of Chih's shoulders, nodding with professional satisfaction.

"—and, of course, I shaved the four Gao brothers, the bandits of the Carcanet Mountains, but that was after they were dead. Give it a feel there, see if I missed a spot."

Obediently, Chih ran their hand over their head, marveling at the smooth skin that replaced the inch or so of growth that had sprouted since they left the Singing Hills abbey early in the spring. The tent was littered with greasy bits of black hair, and their scalp was silky smooth and perfumed with a touch of jasmine oil.

"Now, you'll want to wear a scarf or a hat over that. It's not used to the sun anymore," the barber recited, and Chih nodded.

"I know, thank you. But what were you saying about the four bandit brothers?"

"They tried to poison some imperial inspector, and she tricked them into eating the poison instead," the barber said dismissively, glancing over through the open tent flap at a shaggy man carrying a load on his back. The short woman accompanying him, her own hair impeccably coiffed despite her traveling clothes, made a *hurry up* gesture, and the barber nodded to her.

"Right away, ma'am," he said.

Chih found themself gently pushed outside the tent where a rufous-striped bird hooted gently from a nearby hitching post and fluttered over to settle on their shoulder.

"There," Almost Brilliant said with some satisfaction. "Now you look like a proper cleric again."

"I'm exactly what a proper cleric looks like. Do you know anything about the Gao brothers, bandits in the Carcanet Mountains? Ate poison they intended for a female imperial inspector?"

"I cannot say that I do. Should you go back for the story and to have your brows threaded as well? They're getting rather—"

"I'll go back when he's less busy, and my brows are fine. Anyway, I'd rather spend my money on some lunch than on the privilege of crying in a barber's chair."

"If I had eyebrows, they would be perfect arches, just

like the doorways of Singing Hills," Almost Brilliant grumbled. "But I suppose you must have your treats."

"Your eyebrows would rival the path of the moon itself," Chih said gallantly, heading for the inn that they had spotted coming in to town.

"Flattery, cleric," Almost Brilliant said primly, but she didn't protest when Chih pushed open the curtains that hung over the door of the Running Fox. Unlike the timbered buildings on the street, the Fox was built up from stone, and Chih wondered where the stone had come from, whether it was scavenged from some other place or if it was a remnant older than the rest of the village.

Inside, the Fox was clearly undergoing some kind of renovation. There was a pair of workmen in the scaffolding leading up to the roped-off loft section and a layer of sawdust coming down to cover everything that wasn't sheltered under a suspended cloth or being aggressively wiped down by the waitress.

"Over there under the tarp, please, cleric," she said. "We've got tea and fried bread for now, and if you wait just a little, we'll have some chicken chao as well."

"Tea for now, and I'll have the fried bread with the chao whenever that's up, please."

There were two young women at the table opposite the one Chih took, so different that they couldn't even have been mistress and servant. The smaller woman was dressed in light silk robes in pale blue, her long hair swept up by a small brassy cornet and allowed to stream loose down her back. She sipped at her earthenware teacup as reverently as if it were a sacred elixir, and she sat with her back as straight as the iron pillar at Wei, scorning to touch anything as common as the back of her chair.

Her companion, on the other hand, was ready for the field with the ends of her plain hemp robes hitched up to her belt. She sat with her sandaled bare feet tucked into the rungs of her chair, and she leaned forward with one arm on the table, dipping the end of a fried breadstick into her tea and eating it in large bites.

Despite their differences, the two seemed entirely at ease, and as they waited for their own food Chih watched them curiously out of the corner of their eye.

"We could follow the ox road to An-ti and take a barge downriver," mused the girl in hemp. "I wouldn't mind a while to kick back on a barge and watch the riverlands go by."

"Oh, but sister, that would take so much longer, six days or so at least. It would be faster to take the foot road immediately west, and then we wouldn't need to pay for the barge. Were you not saying that we must be thrifty only last night?"

"I notice that you're only worried about thrift, sis, when there's a water crossing involved. I promise, the Huan River is big and slow as an old sow, it won't be like the storms you're used to."

The girl in silk opened her mouth to reply, but a crashing sound brought her up short. Almost Brilliant peeped in surprise, exploding in frantic wings to sit up on the edge of the tarp, and when they turned, Chih saw what they guessed was their tea splashed on the chest of a large man in the leather clothes of a miner. The man was roughly the shape of a boulder himself, and in his hand, the waitress's wrist looked as delicate as a flower stem.

"Watch where you're going, what kind of place is this?" the man growled, giving her a brisk shake. "You think you get to go running around like this is the damned circus?"

"I said I was sorry," the waitress protested, trying to jerk back, but the man refused to let her go, shaking his head and snorting like a bull getting ready to charge.

"You can't treat people like that," he said, and even before Almost Brilliant called with growing alarm, Chih stood up, smiling and opening their hands.

"Ah, actually, given that it was my tea, I feel that I have cause to be upset here as well," they said, approaching the tense pair. "Why don't you let the young miss go get us both some more tea, and then I can help you get cleaned up?"

Up close, the man was even larger than he looked from a distance, but Chih ignored their instinctive urge to pull back. Their shaved head and indigo robes screamed *cleric* in almost every corner of the empire, and no one really needed to know that the Singing Hills abbey was more about history than it was about religion and common aid.

"Why don't you get us a round of dark smoky tea, my dear?" Chih continued brightly, turning to the waitress and ignoring the man's glower. "Something nice and hot, and I'll get this fine man cleaned up."

The miner's grasp loosened on the waitress's wrist, and Chih was just congratulating themself on a neat job when the man turned and shoved them hard in the chest. Chih fell back against one of the tables, the hard edge jabbing painfully into the small of their back.

"Mind your own damned business, stinking jackal-cleric," he snarled, his face going red, and Chih was just beginning to calculate how very badly they might have played this when the young lady in pale blue slammed to her feet.

"How dare you!" she cried, her voice like a clarion chime. "How *dare* you lay hands on a young girl who only tripped, and again, how dare you abuse a cleric, a holy person!"

Chih could practically feel the situation slip sideways on them. If the man wasn't going to be swayed by the kindly intervention of a cleric, the chances he could be moved by a young woman with only outrage on her side were very low.

"Shut up," the man snarled, turning towards her with a maddened gleam in his eye. "Shut up, shut your fucking mouth—"

"Miss," Chih said urgently, "perhaps it would be best if—"

"What barbaric manners, what lack of respect!" the girl said, unheeding. "The beasts of the field act more correctly than you do, and—"

Chih barely sidestepped as the man roared with fury and charged, and whatever good intentions they might have had were soundly ruined as they tripped over a stool and landed flat on their rear. Above them, Almost Brilliant shrilled in panic, and Chih was just regaining their feet when the slender young woman picked up a chair and threw it straight into her attacker's face.

The man howled as a chair leg caught him in the mouth, splitting his lower lip and sending a shower of blood flying, but he lunged towards her again. Chih stepped back, because whatever was happening was well beyond their scant authority as a historian or a spiritual adviser, and a firm hand grabbed the sleeve of their robe, hauling them back and towards the curtained doorway to the kitchen.

"Welcome to the riverlands, cleric," said the waitress with grim amusement. "You need to learn when to let your tea go."

She dragged Chih into the kitchen where a tired cook was chopping up a thumb of ginger while occasionally stirring a large pot of boiling rice.

"What's happening?"

The waitress only rolled her eyes, pouring them a fresh cup of tea.

"If the big fucker wins, we're probably in trouble, but that's not going to happen."

Chih took the tea—smoky and dark like they had been hoping for—and peeked through the curtains at the mayhem sweeping the front room.

The big man and the young lady had smashed their way through one of the tables and two more chairs, leaving the floor littered with wreckage. The man clutched his arm and reeled back to the center of the inn, bawling curses that echoed off the high rafters. To Chih, this would be the perfect time to make themself scarce, but the young lady only closed the distance, her fists clenched.

"What impudence!" she said, with the kind of diction that could get away with saying things like *impudence*. "People who abuse those smaller and weaker than themselves deserve the lowest, cruelest halls of the dead king!"

He took another swing at her, a right hook that wound all the way back and came forward with enough force to level a city. It would have broken the young lady's skull to pieces if she was there when it landed, but of course she wasn't. In a swirl of silk like a storm, the young lady leaped into the air, throwing the end of her stole over a rafter and lofting herself up like an acrobat.

The man, propelled by his own uninterrupted rhythm, grunted as he lurched forward, and delicately, the young lady's pointed foot pushed off his shoulder, swinging her back. When she swung forward again, it was with all her weight behind her heels, directed perfectly at the man's head.

He went down like a felled tree, practically shaking the inn to its foundations. The young lady calmly let go of her stole, coming to land with a feather's grace on his chest. Her face was still but there was something restless about her eyes that made Chih think of hunting hawks, of endless hunger and winter-sharp ferocity.

"So," Chih found themself saying, "do we clap, or do we run?"

The waitress patted them on the shoulder.

"Well, now Hien and I need to remove the big fucker from the floor. You can go have a seat, cleric. Your food should be out in just a bit."

The young lady stepped down graciously as the waitress and the cook went to drag the man out the door. He was whimpering now through a broken mouth and a nose that was already starting to swell to enormous proportions, and he went without protest. Chih stepped out into the main room, and Almost Brilliant alighted on their shoulder, her claws digging harder into their skin than usual.

"Southern Monkey," Almost Brilliant hissed quietly, and Chih blinked at them.

"What?"

"That was Southern Monkey style," Almost Brilliant insisted as if Chih had tried to argue. "The thing with her stole, my mother saw it in the Verdant Islands, I would swear to it. There were only eighteen practitioners of Southern Monkey style eighty years ago, and nine of them were in their early hundreds. It is *absolutely* Southern Monkey style."

"Do you want me to get you her autograph?" Chih asked, biting back a smile, and got a swift retributive peck to their earlobe for their humor.

Deprived of her prey, the young lady had returned to her table, sitting back down to her tea even as her companion pulled out a worn leather pouch to count out some coins.

"Well, at least it was only a few chairs and tables this time," she said. "And this stuff looks pretty old at that, so let's see, ten and a quarter should cover it . . ."

"Are they going to make you pay damages?" asked Chih, taking a seat at their own table with their tea.

"Of course they won't. They're too afraid that Lady Heavyweight here will bring the place down around their ears if they piss her off."

"And of course we will pay the damages," said the young lady serenely. "We move through this world only with the grace of others, and we must pass without the least ripple."

"No ripples, but broken chairs and broken heads, those are fine. We were trying to keep a low profile, sis."

"Who is going to talk about a little lunchtime disagreement? That is all it was."

The girl in hemp looked like she wanted to argue, but then she shook her head, giving up for the moment to turn to Chih.

"Are you all right, cleric? You took a pretty hard fall. Nice try on stopping things from getting out of hand, though."

"Thank you, and I'm fine, just a little sore and a little foolish. I'm Cleric Chih from the Singing Hills abbey, and this is my companion, Almost Brilliant."

Chih opened their palm so that Almost Brilliant could hop down to perch on it, sweeping her wings open and tocking her head in a small and utterly unhumble bow.

"My pleasure," she said, and both women blinked at her speech.

"Oh, a neixin," the young lady in silk said. "Then you must be a scholar as well as a cleric."

"Say rather a historian and observer, and I have certainly observed a wonder today. May I ask for your names?"

The young lady rose immediately to her feet, clasping her right fist in her hand and bowing low. It was a martial form of deference, and Chih belatedly stumbled to their own feet to return with a bow of their own.

"Honored cleric, I am Wei Jintai of the Fengxi Wei in the Verdant Islands, martial daughter of Yo Laozi."

While still bowed, Wei Jintai lifted her foot and gently mule-kicked the chair that her companion sat on, bringing her reluctantly to her feet as well. The other woman bowed curtly.

"I'm Sang," she said diffidently. "I'm just here to manage the money."

Wei Jintai straightened up, frowning with irritation.

"This is my sworn sister, Mac Sang," she said. "Please, mistress neixin, if you remember us unworthy wanderers at all, please remember that."

"It is my duty and my honor, Wei Jintai," chirped Almost Brilliant, and only Chih knew her well enough to see how she was practically quivering with delight.

"She does a great deal more than hold the purse strings," Wei Jintai said almost anxiously. "She is more clever than a barrow of foxes. She once retrieved a colony of silkworms from the foreigners who had stolen them, and then—"

"Ah, the cleric doesn't want to hear about that, sis," said Sang in a way that made Chih wonder what had happened to the silkworms after they were retrieved. Silkworms in Anh could only be owned by the nobles, and the finer varieties, the ones that spun gold thread and celadon thread and plum-colored thread, were guarded as obsessively as eligible daughters. It had been a real scandal when undyed green silk from the Verdant Islands appeared on the market last year.

"I would love to hear whatever you had to tell me," they said diplomatically, but before anyone could say

NGHI VO

anything else, the curtains over the exit swung open again and a middle-aged couple came in. The woman walked slightly ahead of the man, and Chih recognized them as the pair from the barber's tent.

"Frogs and trees, what in the world is all of this?" the woman exclaimed, toeing a chair leg out of her path. "Is there not one inn in all the riverlands that can keep a tidy common room?"

The man behind her, better groomed now, shrugged, but before he could say anything, the woman's censorious gaze landed on the three of them in the sheltered seating area. She was perhaps in her mid-forties, and Chih instinctively sat up straighter. Out of the corner of their eye, they could see Wei Jintai and Sang do the same.

"You three," she said, pointing at them imperiously. "Are you responsible for all of this mayhem?"

Wei Jintai came to her feet, dipping again into a bow, more humbly this time.

"I am, in fact, responsible for the wreckage, madame—"

"Actually, she's not," said Sang firmly. "Some miner was harassing the waitress, and my sworn sister corrected him."

"And you, cleric?" the woman asked, turning her gaze to Chih.

"She has the right of it," Chih said politely, and Almost Brilliant whistled in assent.

"She dealt most splendidly with the miscreant," Al-

14

most Brilliant declared, making the woman do a quick double-take. "He will not soon be troubling other innocent waitstaff."

The woman scrutinized them for another moment, every inch a teacher who might have them writing lines until dinner, and then she nodded with satisfaction.

"All right, then," she said. "I suppose you're not the lawless bandits I might have taken you for. Now come on. This debris isn't going to clear itself."

Such was her force that Sang, Wei Jintai, and Chih all stood up from their tables to help the woman and her companion tidy away the wreckage of Wei Jintai's fight, setting aside the chairs that might be salvaged, piling the parts that couldn't by the hearth, and hauling the broken tables outside.

The waitress returned in the middle of their tidying, had a few quick words with the woman in charge, and disappeared into the back. When they were just about done, she came back out with bowls of chicken chao for everyone and a bundle of hot fried bread cut into wands as well as a heaping pile of herbs and bean sprouts to cool it all down. The woman who had overseen the cleaning dimpled in delight at the food, paying the waitress from her embroidered purse as Wei Jintai rose in protest.

"Madame, no, please, I cannot permit you to pay for—"

"Ah, silly girl, sit down, sit down, you are only a thousand years too young to play that game with me—!"

Sang, seated next to Chih, snorted softly.

"Auntie versus martial genius, no contest," she muttered.

"I'm a cleric, I try not to pay for my own food," Chih said serenely.

Sang was right about the winner of this particular fight, and the table got down to the serious business of eating the food that had been laid out for them, which was worth their undivided attention. Chih spooned out a small portion of rice in chicken broth for Almost Brilliant, who perched politely on the edge of the table to peck at it, making the woman's quiet companion give her a thoughtful look.

"Enchanted princess?" he asked, and Almost Brilliant preened in delight.

"No, I am Almost Brilliant, neixin from the Singing Hills abbey and descendant of Ever Victorious and Always Kind. My cleric companion is called Chih."

"Aah, what savagery, we've not even given our names. You can call me Lao Bingyi, and of course this old man is Mac Khanh. Who are you kids?"

Wei Jintai repeated her pedigree, suitably impressing Lao Bingyi, and Khanh tilted his head at Sang's name.

"Do you have people up by the Ko-anam Ford?" he asked curiously. "That's where I'm from originally."

Sang looked startled to be receiving any conversation at all, fiddling with her bread before answering.

"No, but my brother was headed up that way a few years ago. Sis and I met in Kochin, where I'm from."

"Oh, you've come a long way," said Lao Bingyi admiringly. "Where are you two young ladies going, anyway?"

It turned out that Sang and Wei Jintai were headed to Betony Docks, one of the river towns that offered transport to points further west. Chih was headed the same way, hoping to catch up with a stipend that was waiting for them from Singing Hills before they took the ferry towards Vihn.

"But really, I'm hoping to spend at least a little while in Betony Docks learning about the local stories and the heroes," Chih said. "The whole world talks about the martial legends that come out of the riverlands, and I would like to see what the riverlands might want to say if they were asked."

"You're welcome to come with us, cleric," Sang said. "The ferry takes less money if we're in a group anyway."

"Why, nonsense," Lao Bingyi exclaimed. "That's an extra four days, and what, all so that a ferryman can drink away your fares? No, come west with us instead on the foot road. It'll be faster by far."

Sang frowned.

"Pardon me, auntie, but we've heard the foot road is more treacherous, and that the ferry is safer."

Lao Bingyi smiled as if Sang had said something funny.

"Listen, my old man and I have lived at Betony Docks since the rocks were soft, and we'd be ashamed to take the ferry. The bandits know better than to raid in this region, and the ones who don't are quickly taught. We'd never hold our heads up again if they saw us floating into town!"

Wei Jintai's head came up, and there was a glint in her eyes as she took Sang's hand.

"If they are not going to take the ferry, then why should we?" she said. "Oh, Sang, of course we must take the foot road. It will be faster—didn't you say we should stay on the back roads?"

Sang hesitated, but before Chih could wonder too much what her resistance was, she shrugged.

"All right. The foot road it is, and if we get our throats slit by bandits or crushed in a rockslide, don't come crying to me."

"Wrong season for rockslides," Khanh said, mopping up the last of his chao with a piece of fried bread.

"Well, there we are then," Chih said.

Chapter Two

The riverlands properly belonged to Anh, but the network of valleys and rivers wove in on themselves like a banker's knot, confounding all but the locals. As their group started to ascend into the hills at the border, the road thinned to a narrow track, wide enough to allow two people to walk abreast if they held hands, but not much more.

"It used to be better," Lao Bingyi said, her lips pursed with irritation. "You know, there was a time when the empress cared about things like the roads out here in the west, back when she first came to sit on the throne. I suppose she's too grand for that kind of thing now."

"You were young in those days," Khanh said with the peaceful air of someone who has said the same thing many times. "The road was bigger because you were smaller."

"Ah, listen to you. I was born as big as the mountain, and I never change."

"Has the area changed very much since you were young, auntie?" asked Chih politely, because they could no more leave a discussion of local history than they could resist a free meal.

"Oh, you know, the officials actually listened to the people, everyone gave generously to the temples, and children surely respected their elders," she said airily.

"It's safer than it used to be," Khanh offered, and Lao Bingyi nodded.

"It surely is that," she said. "Why, straight up to the banks of the Huan River, all of this used to be the territory of bandits and necromancers. Just terrible."

Wei Jintai, walking a little behind, looked up.

"It's true. This was the territory of the Hollow Hand sect," she said.

Chih was opening their mouth to ask about the Hollow Hand sect when Almost Brilliant gave an excited hop on their shoulder.

"Oh, the Hollow Hand! My mother told me about them when I was just a little scrap in the nest!"

"My teacher told me about them as well," said Wei Jintai with a stern look on her face. "She said that they were feared throughout the riverlands for their savagery and their parley with the old ghosts of the Ku Dynasty. He said that they sacrificed travelers on the road for their wicked alchemy, gaining long life and terrible powers."

"My mother told me that they kidnapped young girls who went walking on their own at night, assaulted them, and sold them to brothels," said Sang, sounding bored, and Chih turned to her curiously.

"You sound less than impressed," they said, and Sang shrugged.

"I mean, my mother said that about the sailors from the islands, the musicians from Ue County, and just about everyone who didn't live on our street at home. It doesn't make the Hollow Hand special."

Khanh gave her a disapproving look, but Almost Brilliant fluttered to Chih's other shoulder and then back again.

"My mother said that the Hollow Hand were just as bad as the dead king's brother, more ferocious and more cunning than the bandits of Cao-lun. She said that they could melt into the very mist when the emperor's hunters came, and they fashioned nooses from the clothes of their victims to drag riders from their horses."

"Pah, weaving nooses from old robes, fading into the mist, what criminal can't do that?" asked Lao Bingyi, throwing her hands in the air, and Wei Jintai nodded seriously.

"Truly, they were a blight on the world with their ferocity, but in the end, they were defeated by the Shaking Earth Master."

"The Shaking Earth Master? He's in a few stories I've heard. He was the one who revenged the murder of the

Prince of Lookback Mountain, wasn't he?" asked Chih with interest. Their fingers were itching to transcribe this conversation, but Almost Brilliant's perfect recall would serve for the moment.

Almost Brilliant pecked sharply at Chih's earlobe, remonstrance for some folklore class they had probably slept through or skipped entirely, but Lao Bingyi clapped her hands sharply.

"The Shaking Earth Master! Are you all still telling that story? If you want to talk about ancient history, I'll tell you about when the old governor was meant to pave this road and expand it, and then he spent the money on a dancing boy from the capital instead."

"The Shaking Earth Master and the girl from Taiyuan aren't a story, they're history," protested Wei Jintai, but Lao Bingyi shook her head.

"That silly thing," she said, contemptuous. "People keep wanting to tell old tired stories like that, that's why the world is in such disrepair."

"And why no one goes to temple anymore and children no longer respect their elders?" asked Chih wryly, earning themself another peck from Almost Brilliant and a brisk slap on their arm from Lao Bingyi.

"And why clerics are more interested in free meals and gossip than they are in holiness and correct behavior, I shouldn't wonder," she scolded.

"I beg your pardon, auntie," said Chih, "and I would

be more than happy to hear the story about the governor who was meant to pave this road."

It was actually a pretty good story, and Cleric Dung, who had a special interest in tales of governmental corruption and comeuppance, would be delighted. Chih listened patiently, and then when Lao Bingyi and Khanh were speaking to Sang about some family ties they might have missed, they dropped back to walk beside Wei Jintai.

"So tell me about the Shaking Earth Master and the Hollow Hand," they murmured softly, and the martial artist blinked at them.

"But surely a neixin as wise and worldly about the riverlands knows the story already?"

"I know what my mother told me," Almost Brilliant said before Chih could reply. "I do not know how a young master of the Southern Monkey style would tell it to me."

"Hardly a master," said Wei Jintai with modesty, "and truly, only the most minor student in the long history of the martial world."

Chih waited, and Wei Jintai walked a little slower, letting the others gain some distance from them.

"If auntie is a local, it must still be a bitter pill for her," she whispered. "No matter what the local martial families and sects could do, there was no stopping the Hollow Hand. In those days, they ruled the lower riverlands as fully and as cruelly as any warlord. Auntie jokes, but they really could disappear into the mist, and not just because they knew the land better than anyone else. They had sheared off slivers of their cores and exchanged them for pieces of the old wraiths that live on the mountain-tops. They strung people up like butcher birds, so that all would mark their wickedness."

Wei Jintai shook her head.

"The rule of the Hollow Hand stretched over the riverlands like a shadow, and it was only the Shaking Earth Master who could defeat them. He was the greatest martial arts master in the region at the time, but he had a heart made of stone. He wouldn't move from his fortress unless he was carried forth in a bedecked palanquin. Some reckoned he was just as bad as the Hollow Hand itself if he would sit in his fortress on the river and ignore the cries of the Hollow Hand's victims."

"What moved him?" asked Chih.

"A beautiful maiden from Taiyuan," Wei Jintai said. "She was the daughter of the illustrious Nie family, as beautiful as the moon wreathed in clouds and as accomplished as a dozen Anh courtesans. Her parents sent her east to meet her bridegroom in the city."

She shook her head.

"The processional must have looked quite the prize to the Hollow Hand, and they descended not long after they had come through the pass at Chifeng. They killed the drovers, the guards, and her servants, and they strung them up along the road on both sides, taking her dowry for their own."

Wei Jintai glanced at the group walking ahead, Sang with a slightly embattled look as she tried to complete her family tree to Khanh and Lao Bingyi's satisfaction. When she saw that they were not going to be interrupted, she continued even more softly.

"The girl from Taiyuan, they slit her throat, but they did it badly, cutting her flesh but not her windpipe. They left her for dead under the swinging feet of her own bodyguard, a famed martial artist of the Zhou sect, and she had just enough strength to crawl away in the woods, clinging to life with her fingernails. That was how the Shaking Earth Master found her, in her final gasping breaths and with her throat savaged, and he was so stricken by her plight that he rose up from his own indolence and pride to take a terrible revenge on the Hollow Hand. He went to their lair and challenged them all to battle, the first time he had done a single thing in the martial world for almost a hundred years."

She would have continued but Lao Bingyi called for her, making her straighten guiltily.

"Wei Jintai, Sang says that your mother married into the Wei clan from the northern Shou, and that her teacher was the Scarlet Tern. Come here, tell me, did your mother know Shou Wulai? He would be a tall man, terrible gambler, but he defeated the five Jin Brothers at Port Du . . ."

"Ah, coming, auntie," Wei Jintai said, hurrying forward, and Sang dropped back to walk by Chih in her place.

"So are you two related after all?"

Sang smiled a little wryly.

"Well, my grandfather might have sold one of his relatives some pottery a while ago. It's a little fuzzy, but you know. My family makes good pottery, so I'm hardly in any trouble there. What were you and Wei Jintai whispering about back here while I was trotting out my family tree?"

"Wei Jintai was telling us the story of the girl from Taiyuan and the Shaking Earth Master," Almost Brilliant said. "She was at the part where the Shaking Earth Master went to the Hollow Hand camp to avenge the girl from Taiyuan."

"Hopefully she gets to come back and to tell us what happened next," Chih said, because it looked like Wei Jintai was going to be discussing her cousins on her mother's side for some time.

Sang snorted, shaking her head scornfully.

"Oh, anyone in the riverlands can tell you what came next. Moved by the girl from Taiyuan's beauty, he went and wreaked a terrible revenge on the Hollow Hand, crushing them under the weight of a mountain. Now the area is flattened from his strength, and all the Hollow Hand lie buried under it, nevermore to trouble good people who walk the long roads."

"You like the story less than Wei Jintai does," Chih observed.

"Well, why should I like it? Should a murdered girl only get revenge if she's beautiful? What a cock the Shaking Earth Master must be if he's going to sit on his ass in his fortress, refusing to move until he sees a lovely face and a trim pair of legs."

Almost Brilliant whistled, a slight huffiness in her tone. "Well, it's a very old story," she said. "Things were different then."

"You sound just like Wei Jintai. She says it's all about pity stirred in a cold heart and the triumph that can grow from compassion. I think it's just another dead girl and another martial cock who's too busy reading ancient scripts and lording it over the locals to do any good."

"Are there any stories that you like better?" asked Chih, and Sang flashed them a grin.

"Ones where ugly girls like me get their own revenge? I might have a few."

Sang, it turned out, had several ugly woman stories, tales from the riverlands about female fighters of extraordinary unattractiveness who became legends through feats of martial brilliance. Chih had heard none of them before, and Almost Brilliant only remembered one or two.

"Crying Rock Bao and the Ugly Woman Master were famous in the west river region, and there's of course the stories about women like Wild Pig Yi and Earwig Jing, who are local, but sis and I are from the east. I know them less well."

"You still know a lot, thank you," said Chih, who was looking forward to writing them down from Almost Brilliant's recall later. "I had no idea there were so many."

"Ugly women?" asked Sang in amusement, and they were good enough friends by that point that Chih gave her a quick poke in the shoulder.

"Stories," they said with a laugh. "I'm less educated than Almost Brilliant in the stories of the riverlands, but very few of the stories that I heard had so many women in them, let alone women who were specifically ugly."

"And all the women in the stories that you did hear about were beautiful," Sang said, and Chih nodded.

"At Singing Hills, we do find that most of the women who make it into the archives and histories are called beautiful," they said.

"And in the stories at least, if a woman is not beautiful, then of course she must be ugly if she is there at all," Sang said, rolling her eyes, but then Wei Jintai had dropped back to walk with them, clasping her arm around Sang's waist.

"Are you talking about being ugly again, dear sister?" she exclaimed. "No, how *could* you, you are the most beautiful girl who ever set foot to ground, the most handsome!"

"Augh, sis, get off!" Sang said, squirming against Wei

Jintai's grasp, but as Chih had seen during the fight at the inn, Wei Jintai was very strong.

"No," Wei Jintai insisted. "No, not until you say you are beautiful, because you are, the fairest under the heavens, the most lovely!"

When it looked like Sang was still going to resist, Wei Jintai simply lifted her off her feet. Chih thought of what flowing silk robes might hide, how the cloud of pretty pale blue and white could easily flutter to obscure the form underneath, which was likely more stocky and muscular than might be guessed.

"Say it!" Wei Jintai insisted, coming to a complete stop on the trail, and Sang flailed in indignation. "Say how beautiful you are!"

"Fine, fine, I'm the prettiest teapot in Lady Chu's collection, all right? I'm beautiful, I'm lovely, I'm a delicate flower, now, sis, put me down!"

Satisfied, Wei Jintai set her gently on the road and turned to Chih, bowing deeply before rising with a serious expression in her wide dark eyes.

"Cleric Chih and neixin Almost Brilliant, if you write anything about my beloved sister, you must say correctly that she is beautiful. People must remember how beautiful she is, and how gracious and good."

"I will certainly recall and record what you have said," Chih said with a polite bow of their own, and they would. They would write in their own records, and

Almost Brilliant would remember and pass on to her own chicks how one bright day in late summer, a martial artist called Wei Jintai had asked them to write how lovely her beloved sister was. They would remember the rest as well, and Chih was still hoping to get that story about the silkworm rescue.

Ahead of them, Lao Bingyi clicked her tongue impatiently, and the three of them hurried to keep up.

"Imagine three clever young things like you wasting your time with those old stories like that," she scolded. "Ugly women, beautiful women, what foolishness. Most of us are lucky if we're born with a measure of common sense in our heads."

"Beauty's nice though," said Khanh mildly, and Lao Bingyi gave him a sharp look as well.

"And what would you know about beauty, old man?" she said. "You've been living in the woods since the Emperor of Pine and Steel was a boy."

"I know enough to know I married it," he said in that same measured tone, and to that, Lao Bingyi made her loudest scoffing noise yet, throwing her hands in the air.

"Frogs and trees, I am marching through the woods with three children and an old fool," she exclaimed, but there was the slightest pink blush on her cheeks.

Lao Bingyi didn't hold with stories about the martial heroes at all, but by then she had established a network of kinship ties that at the very edges managed to pull in both Sang and Wei Jintai, and she was pleased to tell them both about it. The sworn brotherhoods and sisterhoods and adoptions of the riverlands could become massively complex and complicated, and Chih was briefly relieved that as a cleric, they were largely spared.

Despite the road west being less than what Lao Bingyi felt it should be, there were still shelters kept up at regular intervals. On the main roads where Chih often traveled, the shelters could be large and accommodating with a regular rotation of food vendors and merchants to keep pilgrims well supplied, but here, it turned out to be just a shed open on one side with directions to a nearby spring carved into a post in front.

"Almost Brilliant and I can go fetch back some water," Chih offered, and Lao Bingyi, who Chih suspected took over management of every endeavor in which she was involved, nodded.

"Thank you, cleric, but take one of the girls with you. No one should wander alone in the riverlands."

"I'll sweep out the shelter," Sang said, gathering up a handful of fallen branches to create a makeshift broom. "We can get this place snug before—"

While still speaking, she had stepped inside the shed, and then she uttered a garbled scream, high and frightened.

Chih spun around as if they had been hauled by a rope, Almost Brilliant squawking with offense and going aloft, but the others were all faster, crowding ahead of Chih to see what Sang had discovered.

"Oh," said Lao Bingyi very softly, and Khanh swore, low and savage. Wei Jintai reached for Sang, gathering her up into the wings of her voluminous silk sleeves, but her eyes were hard and sharp. It was only then that Chih could see the body hung up in the back of the shed, dangling like a gutted hare from the rafters with a white handprint on his chest.

Chapter Three

Sang stumbled from the shed with a gasping sob, as if someone had struck her very hard in the chest, and Wei Jintai followed her, her head still turned towards the shed with a predator's inquisitiveness. Chih, against the rapid drum of their heart, stepped forward to join Lao Bingyi and Khanh.

"The Hollow Hand," Khanh said, his voice remarkably calm, and Lao Bingyi scowled.

"Of course not. The Hollow Hand are dead. Poor imitators. Idiots stealing a monster's mask to make themselves feel worthy. What a sorry mess this is, and this poor young man."

Chih had seen dead bodies before, of course they had. However, death, in their experience, was an old person made as comfortable as they could be, or a cry of anguish during some terrible accident. Sometimes, it was a public execution, handled with pomp and circumstance, the condemned with a white hood over their face so you could never be certain of who it was. Death had a place in their world, even if it was a tragic or regrettable one.

They had never seen a body hung up like this before, rigid and with the hands and face swollen. His clothes had once been very fine, silk dyed a rosy madder, and his traveling shoes looked hardly worn at all. Horribly, Chih found themself thinking that he looked like some kind of decoration, hung up to celebrate a midsummer festival or perhaps some child's name-day and then left behind when all the rest had been taken down.

"We missed the party," they said in a very small voice, and Lao Bingyi gave them a sharp look before nodding.

"We certainly did," she said. "Now come help me, cleric."

"Um, what?" asked Chih blankly, and Lao Bingyi gestured towards the hanging body.

"We need to help him down," she said bluntly. "Khanh is going to cut the rope."

Chih was already shaking their head, their eyes wide, hot, and dry, their hands making vague refusing gestures as if they had been offered food they did not particularly care for.

"Oh, oh, no I can't," they said, a little shrill.

"Of course you can. You're strong enough, believe me, and he needs it more than you need to stand by and stare."

Chih wanted to refuse again, but Khanh, who was already dragging in a sawed stump that was used for seating at the shelter in normal times, nudged them as he went by.

"Do you know what it's like to cut down a hanged body? This is how you find out."

Chih swallowed hard and nodded. They weren't brave, and despite the shaved head and the indigo robes, they weren't particularly virtuous, but more than anything else, they were *curious,* and sometimes that could stand in for the rest.

They came with Lao Bingyi to grasp the hanged man around his waist and one leg. There was a skin-crawling moment where the man's cold hard hand brushed their chest, and up close, there was a smell after all, something musky and choking. Chih grasped the hanged man with Lao Bingyi on the other side, and when Khanh climbed up on the stump to cut the rope, they gasped as the full weight of the body dropped on them.

"Steady, cleric," snapped Lao Bingyi when Chih stumbled, and that helped, the sharpness of her words and the utter lack of surprise or dread in them. To Lao Bingyi, this was one more task that had to be taken care of, like sweeping out the shed or gathering water, and even as a part of Chih's mind cataloged the way the man's silk robes shone in the setting light, and another part screamed in quiet horror, a third part was grateful for Lao Bingyi's pragmatism.

They laid him down on the floor of the shed, and Khanh knelt beside him.

"You left too soon, and that is unfair, but we are not the ones who sped you on your way. Forgive us what we did, and do not follow us when we go."

It was a strange sort of prayer if it was a prayer at all, and Khanh reached into the man's robes before shaking his head and standing.

"No papers and no purse. They robbed him."

Lao Bingyi's lip curled.

"Of course they did. Evil, stupid, and *broke.*"

She turned to herd Chih out of the shed, where Sang was mostly done crying and Wei Jintai still had that terribly inquisitive expression on her face.

"All right, we have a lot to do before dark," Lao Bingyi said. "Cleric, just like before, you get the water and make sure that your bird watches out behind you. Be ready to scream your head off if anyone comes too close, and don't be shy about it either. I'd rather come running because you saw a shadow than otherwise, all right?"

"I don't think screaming is going to be a problem," Chih said shakily, and Lao Bingyi nodded before turning to Sang and Wei Jintai.

"And you two. Firewood and some scouting for good ground. Find him a place to sleep, all right? Soft earth and stones we can pile over him."

Sang and Wei Jintai nodded in unison, and Lao Bingyi

clapped her hands like a restaurant owner giving her staff their marching orders for the day.

"Go on, all of you. There's work to be done before dark."

Almost Brilliant fluttered over Chih's head as they made their way to the spring. It felt as if they were walking a few feet behind where they really were, as if their hands were too far from their body and the ground was both too clear and fuzzy all at once.

Almost Brilliant whistled sharply, bringing them to a halt.

"What?" they asked blankly. "I have to fetch some water."

"I think you should touch that tree over there."

"What, this one?"

They laid their hand against the tree beside them, and Almost Brilliant came to perch on their head.

"What sort of tree is it?" she asked, and Chih concentrated.

"It's . . . got white smooth bark. It's about as thick around as my thigh. It's got black stripes dashed along its trunk, and the branches grow at a tight upward angle. The leaves are a deep green, oval and thick."

"That is good. What else?"

"It's a poplar," they said more confidently. "I don't know what kind, but there are many trees like this here. Poplars have both mothers and fathers, and they will populate a valley with their entire families, rooting out weaker trees and sometimes even older trees with their advance."

As they spoke, they returned to their body, and the world looked the proper distance away, neither too close nor too far. They nodded with relief.

"Thank you," they said.

"What are you thanking me for? I am only doing my job."

Still she came to perch briefly on Chih's shoulder before fluttering up to glide from branch to branch above them, and Chih made their way to the water.

There were two buckets waiting at the spring and a whittled yoke left there to carry the water back. In another time, Chih would have been very curious over the people who had carved their names into the yoke's shaft, a kind of guest log for the shelter, but now they only filled the buckets and made their way back quickly.

By the time they returned, Sang and Wei Jintai had found a place to bury the poor man they had found, and Lao Bingyi and Khanh were digging a grave for him. They hit rock too soon to make it very deep, and after Lao Bingyi had washed the man's face and hands with the water, they laid him in it with a cloth provided by Khanh to cover his face.

Chih realized that everyone was looking at them as the man lay in his sad grave, and they hastily straightened up. They wanted to say that they weren't really that type of cleric; Singing Hills tended to stand apart from the other abbeys in Anh for a number of reasons, and their work had a great deal more to do with history and politics than it ever did with easing the passage from life to death or ministering to the spirits of people on either side of that divide.

From the expectant looks from Lao Bingyi and Khanh and the troubled looks on Wei Jintai and Sang's faces, however, they knew that wouldn't do, and they took a deep breath.

"We commit ourselves to the virtue and mercy of a thousand hands—"

It was hard to go wrong with a prayer to the Lady of the Thousand Hands, and it worked here, for all they had no idea who the man in the grave was. Very few people couldn't get behind the idea of a goddess of profound sacrifice and mercy, and by the fifth round of chanted praises, Sang and Wei Jintai looked a little easier and Khanh and Lao Bingyi murmured in satisfaction.

Chih felt a little as if they had passed a test when they finished, and Lao Bingyi nodded.

"All right. Khanh and I are going to get a fire and some food going. You three can build a cairn, can't you?"

None of them wanted to, but they did it. The first layer of raw stone on the man's body was dreadful, and Chih gained a new kind of appreciation for the tradition of covering the faces of the dead. Then it was just more work, gathering stones to cover the man's body, a chore because if it was more than that, they might sit down to shake and never stand up again.

The shadows were very long and the sky turned to a dim orange by the time Chih, Sang, and Wei Jintai sat down by the fire. A small pot of stock had been prepared with a few balls of cooked rice mixed with dried longfish shreds dropped in.

"Ah, if I knew I would be feeding so many, I would have bought more in town," Lao Bingyi said, shaking her head, and of course Wei Jintai and Sang assured her that it was plenty, it was delicious. Chih, as a cleric who was technically due free meals wherever they went, only thanked Lao Bingyi for her generosity, but they reflected that it was better to engage in this kind of almost scripted exchange than to sit in silence and to think about the poor man who lay in his grave not so far away.

No one was incredibly happy to sleep in the shelter where they had found the murdered man, but as Khanh pointed out, he wasn't in there any longer.

"He's all the way over there in that copse of ash trees," Khanh said practically. "If he comes this way, we'll hear him rustling through the bushes."

"Why would you point that out?" asked Lao Bingyi, aggrieved. "What a grim thing to imagine!"

Before they lay down, Chih hung a string of blessed holy bells across the entrance to the shed, and they went to make sure that Almost Brilliant was snug in the tree that she had chosen. Cuddled against the trunk and fluffed up until she was very round, she was almost invisible in the darkness, and when Chih came to check on her, she chirped at them sleepily.

"If you are murdered in the night, I will tell the Divine that you died well and bravely."

"Thank you for always telling the nicest lies about me."

They set a watch for the night, though Wei Jintai said she could sit for the whole thing and be none the worse for wear in the morning.

"What a silly thing to do when it is so much healthier to only be short a little sleep than a full night's. No one is doubting your mettle, young master Wei, but I expect you to lie down without a fuss when I come to stand my watch," said Lao Bingyi, and with a huff, Wei Jintai went to walk the perimeter with her sword cradled in her arms. Chih hadn't even noticed she had a sword, and they thought again that silk robes like that could hide a great deal.

Chih was fortunate enough to be assigned the last shift before dawn, but their dreams were troubled with visions of the man they had buried, not him as he was dead, but him as he was alive, walking through his life, tending his affairs and all without knowing that there was a white handprint pressed to his chest.

They woke with a start, making Sang who was sleeping at their back grunt in irritation without waking up. Carefully, they disentangled themself from the blankets to go sit with Khanh at the banked fire.

"You can sleep a little longer," he murmured. "I'm good for a while yet."

"I don't think I'm getting any more sleep tonight," Chih said, settling on one of the stumps with their blanket wrapped around them. "Has it been quiet since you've been up?"

"Nothing terrible," Khanh said peaceably, and Chih smiled at him.

"Not much for talking, are you?"

"Oh, I talk plenty when I think I need to. And you. Do you ever stop working?"

"Why should I, when my work is to hear people's favorite stories?" asked Chih, feeling some of the chill of their restless dreams shake away.

"Favorite stories, hm," said Khanh, crossing his arms over his broad chest thoughtfully. "I heard you trading stories with the girls earlier. Thought I heard you mention Wild Pig Yi."

"Yes. Sang was telling me some ugly woman stories, but she said that she didn't know that one."

Khanh shook his head with a trace of disapproval.

"What a rude thing to call them," he said. "You scholars, you need boxes for every single thing."

"How else would we carry them?" asked Chih, and Khanh grunted in assent. He reminded them suddenly of Cleric Sun back at the abbey, who spoke little but who would tell you the best stories about their past as a pirate queen if you only asked right.

"Well, you know, they didn't call her Wild Pig Yi because she was ugly, and you should get that right," he said. "They called her that because this whole area used to be a hunting preserve for the emperor in the old days. After the empress rose up, she preferred to hunt in the north, white bears and seals, I figure, and no use for the boars that they bred up and released in these forests."

He paused.

"You know anything about wild pigs, cleric?"

"I know they're nothing like the tame pigs that people keep in pens," Chih hazarded. "I know that after a certain size, only the nobility are allowed to hunt them, and that the tusks of the biggest wild pig on record frame the doors of the Savage Hawk Hunting Society in Anh . . ."

Khanh snorted, not unkindly.

"That's not bad," he said. "But wild pigs, well. They were big enough that they got to be gods in the old days. One thing that makes you a god is killing a lot of people, and they surely did that. When foxes turn a hundred, they give the moon a skull and turn into humans, but when wild pigs turn forty, they're big enough that the only thing they want to eat is meat."

Chapter Four

They called her Wild Pig Yi because she grew up wrestling wild pigs for fun. When she was a baby, her father quarreled with her mother, and to hurt her, he took Yi and abandoned her in the forest, assuming she'd be little more than a mouthful for some passing wild pig.

Her family thought she was dead for five years, and then on the sixth, she came back dressed in a pig skin with a lance made from a whole pine tree and a fat sow thrown over her shoulder.

She gave the sow to her mother to roast for her return dinner, and with her lance, she drove her father into the mountains to see if he would do better on the mountain than a baby. He didn't, and he was eaten, and for a while Wild Pig Yi lived with her mother and her mother's family in Chifeng.

She was always a wild one, though, and eventually

her mother came to her and said that she wasn't suited to life in the town of Chifeng.

"Well, then," said Wild Pig Yi, who had never learned the trick of being hurt, "where do I belong instead?"

"You might go to the city and make your money in red shoes in the singsong districts," said her mother. "Or you might put on this old coat from your dead father and join the army. Or perhaps there is some other place for you, but it is not here."

That struck Wild Pig Yi as the most clever thing her mother had said in a while, and so with nothing more than that, she set out from the town, which had never struck her as any sort of prize anyway. By then, she was nineteen, and far more terrible than she had been at five. She marched away from Chifeng and never even thought of looking back.

Instead she found her home on the imperial highways and waterways, falling in with pilgrims and mercenaries and theater people. She found them more welcoming than her mother's family, who had nothing to fear but the tax collectors and one another's sharp tongues. The road people liked her for her strength and her courage, and for her part, she liked riding in their wagons and receiving their money in exchange for only a little bit of brawling when the bandits came looking for easy prey.

Ha, do you know, there are still roads in the riverlands that have stones engraved with her name? They tell about how she defeated such and such bandit chieftain or such and such tiger queen, and they make it sound like such a grand battle, as if she were the master of some sect or other, someone near Perfected and gleaming with virtue.

Instead, she was a brawler to the core, exactly as graceful and powerful as the pigs who they say spared her and raised her up on sow's milk and raw meat. She could gore with her lance as well as a pig could her tusks. She was known to be kind, which you should never confuse with being gracious or beautiful or courteous.

The riverlands have always been a contested territory. How could we avoid such a thing, when we are watered by the Huan River, which bleeds its wealth west to the kingdom of Vihn and which can carry the troops from Anh to our doors in twenty days? Wild pigs, tigers, foxes, they all make their territories across the ones that humans propose, and they'll defend them. Even the northern countries occasionally come down to bite us and make sure we're still too mean for invasion.

We belong to everyone and to no one, and when some bandit sets up as a ruler, the usual response is to call them what they want to be called and then not to cry very much when the next murderer comes in. We don't do well with kings here, or queens, or lords. We have a governor, I believe, who stays very politely behind his men at Mo-Lai Fortress, and we tolerate the mayors because they're mostly concerned with keeping the local roads fixed and the poor fed. They know how patient the riverlands aren't, and so they keep to themselves. Good.

You may imagine that this was a place where Wild Pig Yi felt very much at home, and so she lived on the riverland roads for ten years. She protected the heir to the Phoenix Throne as she returned to claim her maternal title. She defeated the Wild Rock of Anpur in a wrestling match fifty-one throws out of a hundred. With the help of a sly fox girl with eyes painted over her eyes, she broke the Four Dams, an attempt by a wicked governor to starve out the people downriver.

Not long after her thirtieth birthday, she took a commission to guide the palanquin of the Beautiful Nie from west to east, traveling along the Blue Road. These days, that road is very safe, but then, it was little more than a passage between the marshes and the willow copses. The safe stretches of land were marked with pillars set by local engineers, but they would be stolen by wreckers, bandits who guided trade caravans into the marshes and robbed them when they mired in the muck.

Wild Pig Yi took the job in exchange for a pouch of gold dust, a packet of rough rubies, and a chance to look upon the face of Beautiful Nie, which was compared by poets of the time to the moon and to the most beautiful of flowers.

The Nie family guards balked at her insolence, and they might have driven her away and taken their chances with the wreckers and the eating willows and the monsters, but a slender pale hand emerged from the palanquin's shuttered window, beckoning Wild Pig Yi closer.

She approached curiously, and when she had peered a while into the palanquin, she nodded.

"It's as the people say," she said with satisfaction, and pocketing the rubies and the gold, she led them into the riverlands.

The first day they were safe, and the second day they were safe, but on the third day, the moon disappeared to tend to his other wife, and the night filled with a thick and sticky summer darkness. Everything was very still, that kind of restless heat that will make you slow and stupid, and as Beautiful Nie prepared to sleep in the palanquin, Wild Pig Yi took up her place on top of it. The palanquin was big enough that she could stretch out fully on its lacquered green roof, and she gazed up at the bare night sky. From time to time, Beautiful Nie would knock on the roof to ask if all was well, and Wild Pig Yi would knock in return, to say that it was.

She had almost drifted off to sleep when there came a hissing sound, higher than a snake would utter and far crueler. Wild Pig Yi rolled over just in time to avoid the arrow that sank into the roof of the palanquin where she had just lain. Immediately, there came a worried knock, and rolling to the ground, she knocked back.

Wild Pig Yi knew two things just then. The first was that if the bandits were attacking with arrows, the sturdy palanquin was the safest place for Beautiful Nie. The second thing she realized was that if they were shooting arrows, then the guards must be dead or traitor, so so much for them.

Silently she rose to a kneeling position, her lance in her hands. She was a darker spot of night, and immediately a dozen different arrows shot from a dozen different directions, and so very great was her skill that she knocked them all aside, sending them spinning to the ground.

Another knock came from the palanquin, and she knocked back again, because all was well, after all. She was Wild Pig Yi, and arrows shot from the dark were nothing to her.

Another flight of arrows came, and then another, and then when they failed as the first flight had, the bandits fell silent. For a while, they were quiet, and Wild Pig Yi thought that they might have seen the error of their ways and crept off to find better prey.

Just when she was starting to relax, however, a man came out of the trees, his pace slow and deliberate, and in his hands, he held a hammer of the kind they use to drive fence posts, so heavy that he had to drag it along the ground so he would not be exhausted when it came time to use it—

"Gravewraith Chen!" squeaked Almost Brilliant. "It's Gravewraith Chen!"

Chih jumped a mile because they had not realized that Almost Brilliant had awakened to listen, and they said the hoopoe's name in shocked surprise.

"Khanh was telling us a story," they exclaimed, and Almost Brilliant came to perch on Chih's shoulder, tossing her little head like she did when she had done something wrong and didn't care to admit it.

"Everyone knows that it is Gravewraith Chen with the hammer," she said pertly. "He was one of the Thunderous Four who almost brought down the King of Mount Lonefox. He got his name because when they were beaten nearly to death and buried in a deep crevasse that went down to the heart of the mountain, he was the only one who survived to crawl out and enact his terrible revenge."

Chih cleared their throat pointedly, because one of the first rules they learned on the road was that it was exceedingly bad manners to tell someone their own story, and nodded to Khanh.

"Please, I would very much like to hear the rest of

this story," they said hopefully, and Khanh nodded, concealing a smile behind his hand.

"Well, maybe it was Gravewraith Chen after all," he said. "It could have been. You know, in those days, people lived longer than they seem to now. It might very well have been him."

Let's say it was Gravewraith Chen, emerged from his crevasse, and he heaved his hammer up to point it at Wild Pig Yi.

"Leave that cargo to me if you value your life," he said. "I own everything that crosses this part of the riverlands."

"You don't," Wild Pig Yi said. "You own what you can take, and brother, I'm telling you now that you cannot take this."

An anxious knock came from inside the palanquin, and Wild Pig Yi knocked back without taking her eyes off of Gravewraith Chen.

"I do not warn people twice," he said, and Wild Pig Yi grinned at him, showing off her sharp teeth.

"You shouldn't bother warning them once. It takes too long," she said, and they rushed at each other.

It was the clash of lightning striking Maidenhair Tower, it was like the sea returning to its old home in the Nguyen Basin. Lance met hammer, and neither shattered and neither would be cast aside. They pushed against each other, no edges between them to cut, and such was their strength that they dug themselves into the earth.

They sprang back and came at each other again, and this time they struck so hard they dug themselves almost hip deep into the ground. Still neither of them yielded.

The third rush, they struck each other, but neither was killed and neither emerged the victor, and so Wild Pig Yi and Gravewraith Chen beat at each other with their weapons, striking blows so hard that lesser people would have died immediately. Mountains would have shattered under their blows, but still they both stood, though now bloodied and furious.

"You hit like an old grandmother swatting at a fly," Wild Pig Yi declared. "You are so slow the Huan River could run backwards and the emperor could give the realm to the rule of the people and they could breed a wise horse and an honest lawyer before you landed a blow."

"You swing that lance like a dancer with a fan," growled Gravewraith Chen. "Are you planning to seduce the governor of the dead when you arrive in Stone Country?"

They both stood still, catching their breath, and another knock came from inside the palanquin. Wild Pig Yi answered it, all was well as far as she was concerned, and then she rolled her shoulders and struck the butt of her lance on the ground.

"Well? Have you decided to nap instead of fighting me?"

Gravewraith Chen started to answer her, but a flight of arrows fell on them like rain. They struck away the arrows that would have hit them, and Wild Pig Yi glanced at Gravewraith Chen.

"Are your friends too impatient to let you do your job?"

"They're not friends of mine," he said, and Wild Pig Yi made a face. The marauders in the forest had apparently hoped one of them would kill the other, but now they were growing impatient.

"Too many bandits in this part of the world," she said, shaking her head, and then another flight of arrows came, this one harder and faster. They were both struck, her in the thigh, and him in the shoulder, and they both realized the same thing at once. With as many archers as now lurked in the trees, they could not dodge them; the first flight would only drive them into the second.

Wild Pig Yi nodded at the palanquin.

"Help me get it out of here, and I'll give you half," she suggested, and it sounded to Gravewraith Chen that it was better than no prize at all.

Wild Pig Yi took up the forward position, Gravewraith Chen took up the rear, and they ran into the forest, away from the roads, along the darkest paths that Wild Pig Yi knew well. The branches lashed at her face, the arrows rushed around Gravewraith Chen's head, and inside the palanquin, Beautiful Nie was thrown around like an ivory die in a gambler's cup.

The bandits, members of the Hollow Hand sect, chased them through the forest sometimes no more than five or six strides behind. They were not only archers. Among their ranks they counted the foulest murderers of the day. There was an innkeeper who struck lone travelers on the head from behind with a club in order to rob them. There was a man who was truly a tiger, banished from his people in the north for his habit of eating the dead. There were monsters who looked like men, and there were men who became monsters, and they chased Wild Pig Yi and Gravewraith Chen through the forest.

The Hollow Hand sect lost them for a short while along the river, and they cast along both sides like hounds until they picked up the scent again, two people carrying a third so that their prints were deep, traveling afraid in the dark. The hue and cry went up, the hunt continued.

The Hollow Hand disciples followed the tracks up into the cliffs, and by starlight, they came to the narrow edge of a steep ledge, looking down over a deep ravine. At the bottom of the ravine, there was the shattered wreckage of the palanquin, but no sign of Gravewraith Chen, Wild Pig Yi, or their precious cargo.

Then from the woods behind them, they heard two cheerful voices singing the old market song.

"My black hen laid eighteen eggs,
Eighteen eggs, eighteen eggs,
I'll cry if I drop even one!"

The eighteen wicked disciples spun around, but it was too late, because the two fighters were among them, too close for their archers or their superior numbers to do any good.

With lance and hammer, Gravewraith Chen and Wild Pig Yi tore through the ranks of the Hollow Hand, and every time they heaved another disciple over the edge of the cliff to shatter on the rocks below, they sang again,

"My black hen laid seven eggs,
Seven eggs, seven eggs,
I'll cry if I drop even one!"

When the final egg cracked on the ground below, they turned to each other warily.

"One more egg," Wild Pig Yi said, but Gravewraith Chen shook his head.

"Not an egg or an enemy, but instead a friend," he insisted. "We have fought with one another, and we have fought side by side. What is left for us but to be friends and sworn to each other?"

"And what is left for the poor thing who came up with the plan in the first place?" asked Beautiful Nie, who sat composed as a lotus blossom at the base of a nearby tree. "What is going to happen to me?"

"Well, whatever you like," said Wild Pig Yi courteously. "Gravewraith Chen and I are sharing you, so he may carry you half the time on the road, and I will carry you the other half, and we shall take you wherever you want to go."

"I thought you were rubies," Gravewaith Chen confessed. "I'm sorry, of course we'll take you where you want to go."

"Well," said Beautiful Nie, "I was going to the capital to serve my family's interests, but the riverlands seem more interesting by far. I think I want to stay with you two and see what may be seen."

That sounded very fine to the other two, and so under the moonless night and over the eighteen dead bodies of the dead Hollow Hand sect, they pledged themselves to one another. They went on to fight other disciples of the Hollow Hand, for the eighteen they defeated were only part of that horde, and other enemies besides, too numerous to name—and if death or betrayal have not torn them apart, why, they must be together still.

Chapter Five

Chih blinked. It was brighter than it had been when they sat down. The air had a bluish cast, and they realized how stiff they had grown sitting in one place for too long.

"I beg your pardon, it is almost dawn, and I have kept you from your sleep," they apologized, but Khanh stood as easily as if he had only been sitting on the veranda of his favorite restaurant.

"Ah, well, you know, at my age, you barely sleep much at all," he said affably.

"And how old is that, uncle?" they asked.

"Oh, you stop keeping count after a while. But when I was a boy, people went to temple and children respected their elders."

"Of course they did," Chih said with a laugh. "Thank you for the story."

Almost Brilliant whistled in agreement. "It was very well told, and so Wild Pig Yi and Gravewraith Chen and Beautiful Nie will live in my memory. I will tell my children of them, and they will never be forgotten."

Chih thought from her formal words that Almost Brilliant must be a little embarrassed from her interruption earlier, but Khanh only nodded.

"Thank you, Mistress Memory. I had hoped so. You said you had heard stories of Gravewraith Chen before?"

"I have. There are not many, but he stands with Lightning Zhou and the Wu Siblings as some of the greatest martial arts masters of their age."

"Hm. Yes. I am glad that I told you this story. It wouldn't be right to have Gravewraith Chen without Wild Pig Yi and Beautiful Nie, I think. They're my favorites."

He shook his head.

"I'm off to cuddle my wife before she wakes up and tells me I am foolish," Khanh said cheerfully. "Call if you need anything."

Chih kept the final watch until dawn, huddled under their blanket with Almost Brilliant dozing on their shoulder. It was a lonely kind of duty, and when they felt themself start to nod, more from boredom than from weariness, they stood to walk around the camp and sometimes to stand outside the shelter and listen to the breathing of the people within.

Welcome to the riverlands, the waitress had said, and strangely enough, they did feel welcome. They could have grown up with Sang and Wei Jintai at the abbey, and Chih doubted there was a single community in the world that didn't have people who took charge like Lao Bingyi and people who went along peaceably like Khanh.

When Almost Brilliant awoke to find herself some grubs to eat, Chih stopped her before she flew off.

"I didn't know you knew so many riverlands stories," they said softly, "or that you liked them so well."

Almost Brilliant hooted disdainfully.

"I have *many* interests and *many* areas of expertise," she said. "My grandfather came from Tsu, you know."

Singing Hills' sister abbey in Tsu sent a neixin once every few years, and took one back with them when they returned home. It was insurance of a sort, to make sure that the knowledge gathered was replicated in another place. Almost Brilliant was heir to the histories of two continents, and Chih smiled.

"Will you tell me some of the riverlands stories?" asked Chih. "I'm not as well educated as you are."

Almost Brilliant perched on her dignity for another moment, but then she gave a little excited hop.

"I can tell you all about the Wu Siblings. They were three, two brothers and a sister, and though they were imprisoned for a hundred years under the house of their greatest enemy—"

Chih walked the perimeter of the campground until the sun was up, and as they did so, Almost Brilliant, her breakfast forgotten or simply foregone in favor of her favorite stories, told them about the fighters and fools and freaks of the riverlands, who may have lived in truth but certainly lived in fiction.

Lao Bingyi and Khanh roused first, and, letting Sang and Wei Jintai sleep a little longer, they set out a cold breakfast of glutinous rice and dried pork, shredded so fine that it looked like wood shavings.

"We shouldn't dawdle," Lao Bingyi said with a stern look as though they had argued. "Another night on the road, and then we should be home to Betony Docks."

Chih nibbled their rice and dried pork, grateful that no one remembered they were meant to be a vegetarian if they could manage it. It was good, settling in their stomach after a night of restless sleep and a morning of new stories.

Soon enough, Sang and Wei Jintai rose as well to claim their food, and though no one was as well rested as they might have been, they broke camp quickly. Sang and Wei Jintai took the buckets and the yoke back to the water, and Chih went to say one more prayer over the body of the man they had buried the day before.

They repeated the prayer for the Lady of the Thousand Hands, and then they hesitated.

"I'm sorry this is the best I could do," Chih said at

last. "You'll be remembered, and if we can find your people, we will tell them about you. Just. I'm sorry."

They had been given to Singing Hills at the age of two. They didn't remember a time when they hadn't been asked to see and to remember, to recite back with accuracy and to ask for the truth in whatever form it came in. Along with the food they ate, they took in the knowledge of how important their work was. This was perhaps one of the few times they had ever thought about how little it all might mean.

Chih turned and nearly shrieked in surprise at Lao Bingyi, who stood watching them nearby.

"You did the best you could," she said practically. "He's safe in the ground, not swinging like they left him."

"It doesn't look very safe to me," Chih said, glancing down at the stones, and to their surprise, Lao Bingyi gave them a one-armed hug, guiding them firmly away from the grave.

"Safer than we are," she said. "Come on. We're wasting the daylight."

When the campsite was put to rights, they set off down the road again, a grimmer group than they had been before. Almost Brilliant alternated between fluttering from branch to branch and resting for short intervals on Chih's shoulder, but she was too restless to stay long.

The road took a slant downwards, and the ground softened under Chih's feet. They were descending into a valley, and the light dimmed around them, giving the trees long and menacing shadows. When it came time for lunch, by tacit agreement, they ate walking, and Almost Brilliant came to perch on the back of Chih's pack, chirruping anxiously.

"It's too quiet," she said. "The birds fled this place. I wish I knew what they had seen."

"You could talk to them?" asked Sang curiously, and Almost Brilliant made an irritated sound.

"Of course not," she said. "I'm a neixin, not a bird."

It was, in fact, a matter of some debate, one in which Chih privately decided to believe whatever Almost Brilliant did, but it didn't seem like the right time to go into it. There was a tension to the valley that hadn't been there before, and it made the muscles at the back of their neck ache, as if at every moment they were resisting the urge to look around and see what was behind them.

Sometime after lunch, Lao Bingyi groaned, shaking her head.

"I swear, this path only gets worse and worse every time I walk it. You know when I was a young girl I could run up and down a mountain carrying my pack as if it was nothing? Frogs and trees, what I would not give to be that young again."

It took Chih a moment to catch on, but Sang no time at all.

"Here, let me help you with that, auntie. Look, I'm barely carrying anything at all . . ."

There was a standard back and forth, *oh, you couldn't* and *no, see, I'm already taking it,* and then Sang and Chih split Lao Bingyi's pack between their own loads. Wei Jintai would have taken some as well, but Khanh was fussing at her about her pack arrangement, something about distributing weight badly and it having consequences later on in life.

"Now you must be very careful with my things," Lao Bingyi said when they were resettled. "Those are supplies we went a long way to get and presents for my family besides, all right?"

"Of course, auntie," said Sang and Chih in near chorus, and they glanced at each other.

"Some instincts never die, huh, Cleric Chih?"

"The world is built on who carries what and for who," Chih said, settling the weight more comfortably on their shoulders. "It's not a bad world where we carry presents for people who feed us."

"It is very important that nothing gets broken," Lao Bingyi repeated. "I will be so sad if those things come to harm, so you must walk at the center of the road, all right? Where it's straight and where you won't trip."

"Ha, you underestimate me, auntie, I can trip over nothing at all," Sang said, but obligingly she and Chih walked at the center of the road, sticking to the driest spots and the most stable ones.

It was all done so neatly that Chih didn't even realize they were being shielded until Almost Brilliant trilled a frantic alarm, and Lao Bingyi stopped dead in front of them.

"Well, come on if you're coming," she cried out, and the words had barely left her mouth before two figures dropped out of the trees directly on top of her. With another warning shriek, Almost Brilliant flew up into the leaves and now Chih could see forms moving between the tree trunks, still enough to pass as trees at first, but now too obviously people and too many people at that.

Chih and Sang beside them froze in shock, and suddenly the air was filled with shouts. Lao Bingyi threw the two figures off of her, but didn't stay still for them to recover. She followed them down to the ground, dropping her knee hard on one's throat with a sickening crunch and dealing the other a savage blow to the temple with a rock in her fist.

There was a swirl of silk behind them and a flash of steel as well, and Chih spun around to see Wei Jintai leap high into the air, far higher than someone should be able to. It allowed her to rain a furious flurry of kicks down on her attackers, striking one so hard that he dropped immediately. One of his companions tripped over his body, but then Wei Jintai's scarf was in her hands, looping around his neck and pulling him forward with a devastatingly final crack.

She didn't pause to watch the dead man fall, but instead was already turning towards another, the butt of her sword coming forward to slam him in the face.

Apparently Southern Monkey style likes face strikes, thought Chih in appalled fascination.

It was like standing in the eye of the storm, and by the time it was over, probably no more than a count to seventy later, there were a dozen bodies on the path. Sang and Chih clung to each other, because, well, the center of the path was solid and firm, and they weren't going to trip over anything if they stayed there.

At some point, the tide turned, and the bandits who had come out of the trees retreated back into them, or at least they tried. Wei Jintai dropped one who had turned his back to run, and she leaped over him to get another, her sword flashing in the light. She would have chased him straight into the forest if Khanh hadn't cut across her path, herding her back to the road. For a moment, it didn't look like she would go, her eyes locked over his shoulder on the shadows in the trees, but then she returned, coming back to stand by Sang's side.

The silence after the last body dropped was different from the silence that had come before, and Lao Bingyi contemptuously cast aside the staff that one of the attackers had thought to use against her.

"Well?" she shouted. "How smart are you now, eh? Are you going to come back for a try now that we're all tired and worn out?"

Lao Bingyi didn't look worn out, and neither did Wei Jintai or Khanh. Instead there was something about them that shone, something that tugged at the back of Chih's head, down between their shoulders. They imagined that it was what dogs felt when they looked at wolves, a sort of terror that something that looked so much like them was capable of such towering fury and destruction.

"Truce," came a thin and hollow voice from the trees. "Truce to take back our brothers who you have defeated."

"Why?" asked Khanh curiously. "The Hollow Hand let their fellows lie where they'd fallen."

"We will fulfill our promise to our fallen and let them fulfill their promise to us," came the terrible voice again, and Chih shuddered. Somewhere above them, Almost Brilliant held herself apart. She would observe, and if Chih didn't walk off this mountain path, she would fly on, to Betony Docks, to the Sisterhood outpost at Leung, all the way back to Singing Hills if she had to. What happened here would be marked, no matter what came.

"What idiots," Lao Bingyi said furiously. "The Hollow Hand counted sorcerers among their number who could raise the dead and make them walk. What bad imitations you are, bad imitations of fools who died long ago."

Their group withdrew from the road, Lao Bingyi and Khanh watching intently, Wei Jintai bristling as if she still wanted to fight. In the middle of their calm cold shock, Chih could see that Wei Jintai's knuckles were split. The blood dripped from her clenched fist to fall onto the road. She shifted from foot to foot, and Chih thought she might have returned to the fight if Sang hadn't been hanging on to her arm.

The men who came from the forest to collect their fallen moved something like shadows and something like spiders. They threw the fallen, some very still, some still groaning, over their shoulders, and then they were gone into the forest. With their departure, something shifted. The very air seemed to grow lighter, and in the trees, a greenfinch called, a series of melodic chirps followed by a husky trill. The world righted, and Chih took a long breath as Wei Jintai blinked and glanced over at her sworn sister's terror. Suddenly it was impossible to imagine her chasing an enemy into the brush to finish him off as she threw her arms around Sang's shoulders.

"Oh, they're gone now, you must not be afraid," Wei Jintai said anxiously, and Sang knuckled a few tears out of her eyes and pushed Wei Jintai back.

"I'm not afraid, I'm terrified," she said. "Those assholes were the Hollow Hand? Why did they attack us?"

"They're cheap imitations," Lao Bingyi said with a toss of her head. "They rise up sometimes, town boys who get it in their heads that they can bring back something great and grand. Just bullies at the bottom of it, and they thought we were easy prey."

That wasn't quite right, Chih thought. The bandits hadn't attacked their party as if they were easy prey. A cleric, two young women, and a middle-aged couple should have been a plum target for bandits, but hardly a challenging one.

That wasn't how they had attacked them at all, and Chih was just chewing on that when Almost Brilliant fluttered back down to Chih's shoulder.

"Oh, that was terrible, I was sure that you would certainly die," she said, pecking at Chih's ear.

"Ow, stop, you're very sharp," Chih protested, leaning their head away.

"I just want to make sure that you're still here," Almost Brilliant said. Chih started to protest again, but Khanh spoke.

"Young master Wei's martial ability is quite brilliant, wouldn't you say, Mistress Memory?" asked Khanh kindly. "Were you able to see her from the trees? As such a devoted fan of the martial arts, I had thought you would be interested in what a genius like her could do."

The genius in question was currently getting her hands cleaned by Sang, who looked a little steadier with something to do. Chih watched them for a moment, and Lao Bingyi went to join them with a little jar of salve from her bag. Even from a distance, Chih could smell the camphor and chili oil in it. It would help, but it would also sting like hornets.

"I'll admit that I was a little too worried about my cleric to watch much," Almost Brilliant said, fluttering to Chih's opposite shoulder. "But I did see that you acquitted yourself quite well, sir. What school or sect do you claim?"

"I wouldn't belong to any sect that would have me as a member," Khanh said, chuckling at his own joke. "You're paying me compliments that I haven't earned in the least. No sect, no master, nothing like that. Just an old brawler who has a few tricks up his sleeve."

He pulled a mean face and took a few exaggerated jabs that were meant to make them laugh, and Chih did, because it was what any old uncle in the village would do for the kids, but still they wondered.

They started walking again, and there was a heightened urgency to it this time, Lao Bingyi in front and Khanh in the rear. The shadows grew longer and colder, and then it was time to stop again, this time without a shelter but also fortunately without a corpse hung up over them.

Dinner was a quiet affair, and as Wei Jintai and Sang settled down to sleep first, Chih pulled out some paper and their writing supplies, curled as close to the fire as they could get with a thin wooden board for a writing desk.

"What are you doing?" asked Lao Bingyi curiously.

"I've been letting my notes get away from me this trip," Chih said with a rueful smile. "Almost Brilliant is amazing, but I cannot depend on her to hold everything for me."

"Of course you can," Almost Brilliant said scornfully. "Seventy neixin like me, and you could transport the whole of the Singing Hills archives across the world in a single flock."

"You're very good," Chih said with a small smile. "I'm really just along to open doors and to make sure people notice you."

Almost Brilliant chirped smugly, and Lao Bingyi leaned in without the least bit of self-consciousness to read what Chih was writing.

"Ha, you're writing about *The Cruel Wife of Master See,* why in the world are you doing that?" she exclaimed.

Khanh, who was doing some stretching exercises by the edge of the fire, looked up in surprise.

"The Cruel Wife of Master See?" he asked. "They're still performing it?"

"Well, that's what the barber back in town said," Chih replied, a little bit defensively. "He said that an actress named Crimson Bow and her company came through, and they were the ones performing it."

"Oh, Crimson Bow from Fenghua," said Lao Bingyi with a snort. "I can imagine how she played it too! *Oooh, the winter wind howls and so does my heart for vengeance and for honor and of course for the millstone's weight of the jewels I'm wearing while doing high kicks on stage!"*

"I just can't believe they're still performing that old thing," Khanh said, shaking his head. "Why don't they get some new plays? They don't have to go back over the old ones again and again. So boring."

"*Oh, my sleeves are heavy with my tears for I cannot stop making every bad decision I can find, and I cannot choose between a decent man and one who corrupted his own core for power and glory!*"

"That barber wasn't much better than a sheep shearer. Couldn't get my hair even for ages, and at the end I think he was just snipping air to shut me up. You're lucky you just went to him for a shaved head, cleric. Hard to mess that one up."

"*Oh no, here comes a mammoth! How did we get a mammoth in the riverlands? Who knows, but now it is trampling everyone flat, too bad, so sad!*"

Chih did chuckle a little at that, because there were perhaps a handful of plays that could get away with a mammoth trampling everyone flat for an ending, and *The Cruel Wife of Master See,* all about the tragic deaths of a riverlands sect master and his beautiful wife, both betrayed by his best friend and his wife's secret lover, was not one of them.

"I saw it performed when I was a child at the abbey," they said. "I thought it was good."

"What you need is to watch some old-fashioned xauhi operas," Lao Bingyi said, rolling herself up in her blankets and settling down beside Sang. "Those are so good that it doesn't matter where they're set or how the actors dress. If you're still in the riverlands by the equinox, they do a festival at Anhui, you should go. *And* you should get some sleep. You have the last watch again."

"Of course," Chih said with a smile, and they wrote as fast as they could, making notes for how Lao Bingyi and Khanh felt about *The Cruel Wife,* before writing down the other stories they had heard over the last few days. Then they tucked their work away and fell into a restless sleep until Khanh came to wake them.

"Were you awake this whole time?" they asked, rubbing at their eyes.

"My wife came to sit with me for a while. You and the girls need your rest, and as I told you before, I don't sleep much."

"Mm, thank you, I like to sleep a lot," Chih said, climbing to their feet. The sky above them was more blue than black, and there was a slight warmth to the air that made it somewhat bearable out of their blankets.

"You and auntie really don't like *The Cruel Wife,* do you?" Chih asked. They had an idea why Khanh and Lao Bingyi might not like the story, and they wanted to give Khanh an opportunity to tell another one, if he wished.

In the darkness, it seemed as if Khanh's eyes were darker still, strange and indifferent to light. They had seen that look in Lao Bingyi's eyes while she was fighting. They guessed that sooner or later, if she kept walking the martial road, Wei Jintai would have it as well.

"Well, you know, it's a matter of taste," Khanh said at last. "I guess there's people out there who think it's a good story or that it's an important one."

"Not you?"

"These days, I think it's hilarious. And she's right, you could do worse than to take in some xauhi opera if you get the chance. That's the good stuff, they don't make them like that anymore, and why would they, when they did it right the first time?"

"Back when everyone went to temple and children respected their elders?"

"Yes, then. And now I really do need to get at least a little sleep, cleric. My wife gets terribly upset if I don't."

"Of course, I am sorry for keeping you from it," Chih said, and when the sky grew lighter and they could see their hand in front of their face again, they took out a sheet of paper and started to write.

Chapter Six

Around true dawn, there was a light drizzle that suffused the trees in mist. It left Chih's clothes clammy, made the tips of their fingers and their nose feel terribly chilled, but there was something bracing about it as well, as if the world had rolled back to an earlier, wilder time.

Lao Bingyi took great gulps of the cool air, squaring her shoulders up and planting her fists on her hips.

"This is why all the great fighters come from the riverlands," she said, slapping Wei Jintai companionably on the shoulder. "Breathe this every day of your life, and you'll fly where others have to crawl."

"That is what my master, Yo Laozi, said as well," said Wei Jintai, and Lao Bingyi nodded.

"She's a wise one, your master. I never met her, but her brother, he was a tough customer when he came to the riverlands. We fought, you know, and then we threw in together for a while . . ."

"How long ago was that, auntie?" asked Chih respectfully, and Lao Bingyi waved them off.

"Oh, it was a while back. Old man, when was that? Had we planted the hawthorns yet?"

"Which ones? We planted the ones on the north bank, and then—"

"Oh, right, right, and then the ones by the edge of the pond as well. My goodness, that's been a while, hasn't it? A while ago, cleric. Now, no more talking about old history. Everyone eat up. If we go quickly we'll be home before sundown."

They went faster than they did the day before. Chih was used to setting their own pace and found that they had to concentrate to keep up, matching their stride to Lao Bingyi's in front. Beside them, Sang sounded as if she were tiring as well, but Wei Jintai's mincing gait, short and smooth so it looked as if she rode on a cloud, would have left them both behind if she did not wish to stay close.

It was Lao Bingyi in the front and Khanh in the rear, but when Chih looked back a short while after they had set out, they were startled to see no sign of him.

"Wait, Khanh's gone—!"

They pictured Khanh hung up in the trees like the poor man at the shelter had been, an image that came so strongly that tears started up in their eyes, but then Khanh popped out of the trees, jogging to catch up.

"Oh, don't worry about me," he said easily. "Just stepping off to do what needs to be done, you know."

"Ah, don't worry about him," called Lao Bingyi from the front. "He's tough as old leather. If they stab him, they'll only lose their swords in his gut."

Chih smiled because they knew that Lao Bingyi and Khanh meant to be comforting, but when they looked back a little later, Khanh was gone again. This time they didn't say anything, and when they counted to a hundred and looked back, he was walking behind them as easily as if he never missed a stride.

A short time after noon, the ground took a much steeper slope, and Chih could hear the rushing of the river below.

"That's the Huan River," Lao Bingyi said with satisfaction. "When it was young and wild, it carved this valley from the earth in four days."

The road switched back and forth, attempting to alleviate the steepness of the descent, and after a turn that looked like any other, they could see down on the river itself, broad and shining, beaded on either side by houses of reddish stone and docks painted pale green and white. On the near bank, there was a large hall built out onto the water, and Lao Bingyi nodded with happiness.

"Home," she said with pleasure. "Girls. Cleric. Welcome to Betony Docks."

It was only when they descended to the valley floor that they heard the cries, shouts of fury and the clang of swords. From where they stood on the road, they could see a roil of people between the houses and the clamor of something that could only be violence.

Even bad imitations can get up the courage to attack, Chih thought numbly. *Even cowards can swing swords . . .*

With a furious cry, Lao Bingyi shrugged off her pack, dropping it to the road. She flew into the fray, each stride seeming to cover more distance until her feet barely touched the ground at all, and hot on her heels was Wei Jintai, her sword drawn and her robes fluttering after her.

Khanh clapped both Chih and Sang on the shoulders.

"You two should stay out here," he said. "That's going to be a mess, isn't it?"

He smiled at them both, and Chih's vision doubled for a moment as they tried to see two things (or perhaps three or four things) at once. Then he was gone, not with the flashing quick steps that Lao Bingyi and Wei Jintai had employed but with the long lope of a wolf that knows to pace himself for a hunt.

"We can't just stay out here," Sang said indignantly, but Chih was already shaking their head.

"If those people came prepared to fight the likes of Lao Bingyi and Mac Khanh, I sincerely doubt we're even going to make them pause," they said, and then they considered.

"Almost Brilliant? Would you go scout for us? Fly over quickly and see if there's anyone who might need our help or anything we could do?"

Almost Brilliant chirped an assent before she took wing, and Chih took a deep breath to calm their nerves. The shouting and the clash of arms made them shake, and the instinct to run away was very strong.

"Is she going to be all right?" asked Sang, and Chih nodded.

"No one stops to kill a little bird during a battle," they said, reminding themself as well. "We have some records, old ones, about how the first neixin were condors and eagles. I've been very glad many times that Almost Brilliant is as small as she is."

Sang nodded distractedly, but her eyes were fixed on what they could see in the village, which wasn't much. Whether the attackers were actually members of the Hollow Hand or simply crude imitators as Lao Bingyi insisted they were, they were dangerous, and they were deadly. Chih's hands shook, and they clasped them together, centering the way they had been taught, grounding themself so that when the time came to act, they could do so.

Are you seeing, really seeing? Cleric Hahn said in their memory. *Will you remember?*

Wei Jintai suddenly appeared on a roof, not as if she

had climbed but as if she had leaped. Two figures in black followed her, circling her like dogs would a bear. She was shorter than both of them, and they bore pole-axes, longer by far than her sword.

Wei Jintai gave no indication that she was meant to be at a disadvantage. Instead she spun in a tight circle to dodge the first lunge and twisted behind her attacker. A flash of her sword, and she skewered them both chest to chest. Chih thought with frozen horror of how much force it took to send a sword straight through two bodies and then to jerk it free again with nothing more than a flick of her wrist.

Another leap put Wei Jintai back in the war again, and slowly, the two bodies she left behind slipped off the roof.

I'll remember that I was terrified, Chih thought. *I'll remember what it was like to see a battle between people who don't fight like people, who are what legends come from.*

"She's so strong and wild her master sent her away," Sang said, something numb in her voice. "She would never be content to do good in the civilized world. She would never fit there, not with the stories they were beginning to tell about her. They were saying such . . . She needed to come out here, to be with people more like her."

The clash of swords, the howls of the dying.

"She belongs here," Sang said, and Chih looked at her.

"And you?"

Before Sang could answer, Almost Brilliant returned, landing on Chih's bare head.

"Ow! Almost Brilliant, get down!"

Almost Brilliant hopped onto their shoulder, but her claws pricked straight through the cloth in her haste.

"There's a hall by the river, built out onto the water. There's wounded there, and children and the elderly."

"Right," Chih said, nodding. "That's where we're going. Sang—"

"Of course I'm going," said Sang, growling to hide the fear in her eyes. "I can't swing a sword, but I'm not useless."

Almost Brilliant guided them in a wide circuit around the fighting, keeping them to the fringes of the trees until they emerged by the river.

The Huan River ran fast here, throwing up waves like horse heads, thundering and flecked with foam. The hall they had seen from above was built on a support of ancient logs, the porch a good ways above the water and connected to land by a long wide staircase and a winding ramp. Even as Chih approached with the sounds of the battle in their ears, they noted that it was a gorgeous structure, tiled with celadon, with shutters elaborately woven from willow withes.

As they hurried up the stairs, Chih laughed suddenly.

"What?" asked Sang.

"This is Ku Dynasty work," Chih said a little giddily.

"No nails, it's all just joined together. It's amazing, really . . ."

Sang groaned.

"Talk about it with Lao Bingyi later. She can probably tell you all about the builder who tried to cheat his fees."

At the top of the stairs, there was a pair of doors carved with a pattern of betony flowers. They barely shook as Sang pounded on them.

"Let us in, we're here to help," she cried.

There was a scrabble behind the doors, the sound of running feet, and then a half-grown boy unbarred the way to let them in.

"Come on," he said urgently. "Come on, this way."

They helped him bar the doors behind them, and then he led them across the large building to the rear, where perhaps thirty people sheltered. As Almost Brilliant had promised, it was the wounded, the young, and the elderly, those most likely to suffer during fighting, those least likely to be capable of defending themselves. There were also a half dozen wounded, stretched out groaning on the ground or lying troublingly still.

Moving among them was a gray-haired man supporting himself with a cane. He gave Sang and Chih a sharp glance as they came in, and then he handed Sang an armful of scrap fabric and pointed her towards the jugs of water.

"Clean and bandage," he said firmly. "If you don't

know how, you'll learn quickly. And cleric, the children, please. Be very sure that you keep them behind the flower line."

Chih glanced down and saw that the floor of the hall was separated by bands of inlay running across the width, dark and light wood set to produce a repeating pattern of flowers. It was a lovely detail, and at the moment, a good way to make sure that the dozen or so children didn't venture too close to the windows along the side or the doors.

Chih had never spent much time in the crèche at Singing Hills, but they knew enough to take the baby away from a terrified ten-year-old and to gather the rest around them at the rear wall.

"Everything looks very scary right now, doesn't it?" asked Chih, cuddling the baby for comfort as much as anything else. "Who's scared?"

The smaller children raised their hands, and a few of the older ones gave Chih unimpressed looks. Chih smiled, taking a seat, and gesturing for them to sit as well.

"Well, I'm very scared," they said truthfully. "And you know, the moon's daughter, Princess Shining, was very afraid as well when the word came that her mother's lands were being devoured bite by bite from east to west. It could only be the Roaring Girl of Whistling Mountain, who was so hungry she could eat a kingdom, so Princess Shining went to meet her. What do you think Princess Shining took with her?"

Almost Brilliant came down from the rafters, perching on Chih's knee.

"I think she brought along her mother's spindle," Almost Brilliant said, and then she fluttered to a little girl with her hair done up in braids. Chih wondered who had braided her hair for her, if they would be around to take the braids down that evening.

"What do *you* think Princess Shining took to meet the Roaring Girl?" asked Almost Brilliant curiously.

"Um. She brought an ox. A big one."

"A big ox," Chih marveled. "How clever of her. So she brought a spindle and an ox, and it was very important that she did so . . ."

Chih didn't spend very much time with children, but they lived in stories, and for a little while, they could invite the children of Betony Docks into the house they made, offering them the fragile shelter of a story they had all built together.

The shelter collapsed with a boom that echoed throughout the hall. The barred doors at the far end buckled, and before anyone could run to shore it up again, they blew open, and a band of marauders in black crowded the entrance, flooding the hall.

Chih clutched the baby tighter, rising to their feet as the man in front, his hair pulled back by a black kerchief and his face nothing but hard lines and anger, stopped the rest.

"Master of Betony Docks, come out and face us."

The gray-haired man with a cane, a pad of bandages still stuck under his arm, looked up from bandaging a young woman.

"You are not worth facing," he said calmly. "Thugs and criminals, bandits who hide under the shrouds of people who were trash even before I destroyed them. A wild pig would offer me more honor in combat."

Almost Brilliant pressed against Chih's throat, shivering, and then she flew up to the rafters, huddled against a beam. Chih would never begrudge her her safety or her function, but they were very cold and suddenly terribly lonely without their friend.

"Come and fight, Master Nie," the man growled. "Come and fight, and we will spare your remnants here."

"You know? I do not think I will," said Master Nie, and the leader of the Hollow Hand's face contorted with rage as he raised his sword.

"Kill them all," he said, and they rushed the infirmary.

Chih had spent their entire life trained to observe and record. Now, in what they were becoming increasingly sure were their last moments, they picked out strange things. They saw how young the Hollow Hand was, boys in their teens and early twenties. They saw how hungry the bandits were for whatever it was their leader had promised them, and how they would kill for it, and how easy it would be for them.

They saw the man with the cane drop it and take two

steps backward, reaching up as if to claw at the air like a cat, and they saw the series of wooden rings hanging from the rafters on fine silk thread, rings that fit his fingers perfectly.

Chih saw how calm Master Nie's face was, not afraid, not furious, but *interested* as he pulled forward and down with all his might, and then the earth shook.

Chih screamed, the baby in their arms screamed, everyone screamed, and they were thrown to their knees as it felt as if the sky must be falling down on their heads.

No, not the sky, just a hundredweight of timber and tile, and that is bad enough, that is all that is necessary, it will break us . . .

That was the image that stuck in Chih's mind as they closed their eyes tight, themself and the remnants of Betony Docks shattered like porcelain dolls, thin bone-white shells spilling their red insides out under a noise that was so thick and crushing and absolute that of course there couldn't be anything left alive.

Then, somehow, they were, and Chih choked on what felt like a lungful of grit. They coughed in surprise that they could still cough, and they opened their eyes only to shut them again against the dust thrown up in the air. Everything had been lost to billows of grit, and the baby in their arms wailed.

Over it all, however, came a booming, rolling laugh, delighted and as out of place as a ship in the desert.

As the dust settled, Chih blinked to find themself outside, sheltered under a pavilion that was all that was left of the hall. Everything behind the flower line was as it had been; everything beyond it was sinking into the water.

Horrified and fascinated, Chih went to the edge to look, and in the mess of logs and tile, they could see the wreckage of what had been the Hollow Hand, crushed, mangled, and now with the river rushing over all.

The baby wailed, and Chih pulled their swaddling over their face to shield them from the dust as they looked up wildly.

"Almost Brilliant? Almost Brilliant!"

For a terrible moment, there was nothing, and then Almost Brilliant came down to their shoulder again, her nails piercing the fabric of Chih's robe entirely.

"What in all the world?" gasped Almost Brilliant, and Chih didn't have anything to tell her.

Master Nie had fallen back to sit on the ground, still laughing with his legs stretched in front of him. Now they could see that one foot was swollen visibly larger than the other one and wrapped in bandages, and one of the women brought him his cane again. When he turned to Chih, his eyes were bright as desert stars.

"A cleric who shows up with a talking bird in times of trouble—*you* must be from Singing Hills."

Chih bowed as best they could while holding a crying baby. They thought their arms were going to cramp in that position, and then they would never be able to put the baby down.

"Master Nie, I am," they said, and he laughed again, a normal one this time.

He climbed to his feet with an impressive economy of motion, leaning heavily on his cane and shaking his head.

"You must tell the world of my cleverness," he said. "You must tell them how I defeated a full twenty enemies with a single fell blow, how the Hollow Hand was destroyed again."

He coughed, and it was that doubled vision again, both a mad architect who had designed a community pavilion as a deadfall trap and the man who had carefully overseen the wounded, the young, and the old.

"And of course," he said with a real vanity that was pretending to be a false vanity, "and of course I would not mind it if you told them how handsome I was while I did it."

Chih suddenly found themself remembering Sang's comment on the road, about ugly women and beautiful women. People were beautiful or ugly because other people said they were, and apparently Master Nie, who had been the Shaking Earth Master and Master See, had decided he liked being Beautiful Nie the best of all.

Their thoughts were interrupted by a thin high whistle drilling straight into their ear.

"Pah! Old man, you left handsome behind with your

thirties, and I do not even like to think how long ago that was!"

Lao Bingyi's voice carried from one of the log pillars braced in the water. It had once supported the hall, and now it stood alone with Lao Bingyi balanced on top of it. Chih realized with impressive calm that she must have leaped from the shore; otherwise, there was no way for her to have made the crossing.

Lao Bingyi had a bruise growing dark on her forehead and her left sleeve was soaked in blood that might have been her own or someone else's, but her pinned braids were still pristine, and she looked mightily put out. She shook her lance at them from across the water.

"I am getting the boats, and we are bringing you back to shore. Do not think you can hide from clean-up by staying on the water and designing your next monstrosity. Cleric, are you well? Is Sang with you?"

Chih blinked to be addressed, and they stepped forward hastily.

"We're both here, and we are both unharmed."

"Good! There's a great deal of work to do!"

There always is, Chih thought wryly, rocking the quieting infant in their arms, and they were relieved they were still around to do it.

Chapter Seven

A skinny woman with a bandaged wrist ferried them back to land in a flat-bottomed fishing boat, poling expertly around the fallen wreckage. When he gained the shore, Master Nie grabbed Lao Bingyi in a one-armed hug, pushing his face against her cheek with an affection so deep that Chih blushed.

"Hello, beautiful one. I've missed you."

"Missed the plumb bobs and books I was bringing back for you, maybe." She snorted. "Look at you, so happy that you finally got to test your toy."

"And who's going to have to put it all back up, I ask you?" said Khanh rhetorically. He had laid his hammer aside to greet the boat, and now he came to press his cheek against Master Nie's and then Lao Bingyi's.

Something passed among the three of them, and beside Chih, Sang whistled softly.

"There's something you don't see every day," she said, and Chih shrugged.

"Sometimes you get told about it," they said thoughtfully. "Maybe you get told about it two or three times, and you just don't know what you're hearing."

"Hm?"

"Come on, I need to find out who this baby belongs to. My arms are going to fall off if I have to keep carrying them."

To Chih's relief, the baby's parents were still alive, and when they gave the baby up, they were immediately pressed into service.

Lao Bingyi wasn't joking about how much work there was to do. There had been deaths, and even as cheaply as life was reckoned in the riverlands, there were people left behind who needed to mourn and to figure out what came next. There were the wounded to tend and the dead to lay out, both the people of Betony Docks and the dead of the Hollow Hand. Even more difficult were the members of the Hollow Hand who had survived, the youngest around fourteen years old, and Chih was grateful that they weren't in charge of what fate waited for them.

The work went on through the evening and into the night, and sometime after the moon was high, Chih was hastily given a bowl of rice with a piece of fatty chicken thrown on top and told that they could sleep at Khanh's house. They collapsed behind a woven willow screen, and when they woke around dawn, they were snuggled up with Sang and Wei Jintai beside them. Wei Jintai's head was bandaged up, the bandage drooping down to cover her right eye, and underneath the cloth wrap, her mouth was pursed childishly in sleep. She looked younger when she slept, especially with how she clung to Sang, and Chih was careful not to disturb them when they rose.

The morning mist rose up from the water, blanketing Betony Docks in soft gray, and even the calls of the early river birds were muted. In the water, the pavilion crouched over the wreckage of the hall and the enemies it had crushed, but besides that, there were no obvious signs of what had come the day before.

They walked down towards the water, and Lao Bingyi met them halfway there, a round basket of oil bottles and lotions balanced on her head and a towel thrown over her arm.

"There's a good spot this way," she said, leading Chih to the shore.

Chih followed her to a sheltered spot upriver where the sand led directly into the water and a spar of rock prevented too many sticks and stones from gathering. Lao Bingyi tsked and gave Chih one of the bottles.

"You got a little burn on your head. You should have covered up more on the walk. Here, rub this on."

Chih obediently smoothed some of the cream on their tender scalp, and they watched out of the corner of their eye as Lao Bingyi matter-of-factly stripped off her clothes and waded into the water. Naked, Lao Bingyi was smaller than she looked clothed, wrinkled and soft over the muscle packed on her frame. There were two gold rings set with rubies piercing her nipples, another through her navel, and ringing her throat like a necklace was a terrible old scar.

She caught Chih looking, and she shook her head.

"Not all stories are worth telling, cleric."

"But it would be your story," Chih said, trying not to insist. "It would be the truth. Wouldn't that be better than—"

"What my story is, cleric, is *mine*. You have the rest, and you'll tell the rest. Be happy with that. My story's mine, and you don't get to have it."

Lao Bingyi shook her head.

"Half of the stories never remember Khanh anyway. They make him a dead bodyguard or a traitor or a fool. They say he's from the Carcanet Mountains or Vinh or Ue County, anything but a nice Viet boy from Ko-anam Ford who doesn't much like to talk about himself. What good is that?"

She turned her muscled back pointedly to Chih, and Chih sighed and gave up, stripping and wading into the water. It was frigid, but they adjusted to it with long breaths until they were submerged up to their shoulders.

Lao Bingyi waded out to settle her basket on the rock

spar, selecting another bottle and using the contents to lather her skin.

"I think Wei Jintai might stay with us a while," she said thoughtfully. "And if we keep Wei Jintai, I have hopes we'll keep Mac Sang as well. She's a likely looking thing. Sensible. We never have enough of that in the riverlands. I know that my old man would love to hear about those silkworms she doesn't want to talk about. It sounds like the kind of thing he would have done before his feet started to hurt.

"They'll tell stories about Wei Jintai if they've not already started," she continued. "You have one now. I imagine you even think it's the truth."

There was something arch and catlike about her tone, and Chih considered before they answered.

"I know what I have seen," Chih said finally. "There's what Almost Brilliant has seen. There's what the people who survive her will say. Auntie, there's what you will say as well."

Lao Bingyi took down her hair, thick and heavy, strikingly black, though whether it was luck or cassia dye that kept it so, Chih couldn't guess. It was easy to imagine the cruel wife of Master See and the girl from Taiyuan with hair like that. Perhaps Wild Pig Yi had hair like that too, but they didn't say such things about her.

"I will be good to her," Lao Bingyi said. "The frogs and trees only know that she will need it. And cleric, what will you say?"

"I'll do my best to be honest," Chih said, and somewhat to their surprise, Lao Bingyi smiled. It was a riverlands thing, feral and strange and certain.

"Good," she said. "And you cannot help being kind. So I suppose that will work itself out."

Chih, raised in the deep archives of Singing Hills since they were two, thought that it would. They tried their best to be kind, but they were also patient. Singing Hills knew that the truth showed up in its own time, often late and sometimes entirely unlooked for. Lao Bingyi was old, and her life might last years, decades, centuries more. Singing Hills was older still.

They could wait.

Acknowledgments

Sometimes, I think it's a little sad that it's impossible to know all of a person, no matter how long you've been together or how well you love them. That's part of what *Into the Riverlands* is about, I think, about how many moving parts go into making a person, and how the stories you're told are only ever going to get you halfway there. It's sort of sad, what you don't know about the people around you. Then you turn around and realize that someone you've known for years is out back riding the unicycle that you never even suspected, and honestly, it can also be a delight.

Similarly delightful are Diana Fox, my agent, and Ruoxi Chen, my editor, who are always asking me the right questions to make sure that my work is saying what I want it to say. Thank you to you both, because this book wouldn't be this book without the two of you, and I wouldn't be the writer I am today.

Thank you as well to the Tordotcom team. You have been amazing to work with, and I can't imagine Chih, Almost Brilliant, and their story with anyone else. To Irene Gallo, Sanaa Ali-Virani, Lauren Hougen, Jim Kapp, Greg Collins, Amanda Hong, Kyle Avery, Alexis

Saarela, Michael Dudding, Isa Caban, Samantha Friedlander, Megan Barnard, Christine Foltzer, and Jess Kiley, thank you so much!

Thank you as well to my cover artist, Alyssa Winans, and my audiobook narrator, Cindy Kay, who tell this story in ways I can't even begin to understand.

To my friends Cris Chingwa, Victoria Coy, Leah Kolman, Amy Lepke, and Meredy Shipp, thank you for everything you do. Wanna get some food after this? I'm kind of feeling like Vietnamese or Thai.

Shane Hochstetler, Grace Palmer, and Carolyn Mulroney, I can't thank you guys enough, and I'm not even going to try anymore. I'm just going to buy you lots of cheese and baked goods and assume it gets the point across.

The world's changed from what it was when I wrote this book in 2021, and it will have changed even more by the time you have it in your hands. Wherever you are, I hope you're okay. I hope you're having fun. I hope you're safe. I promise you I'm doing my best, and if you are too, we just might be okay.